D0063579

Ghosts of Whitner

by

J. A. LeVitt

WITHDRAWN
UTSA Libraries

Ghosts of Whitner

Copyright 2004
by
J. A. LeVitt
Author photo and cover art by Mike LeVitt

ISBN 1-932196-47-1

One Night Books #1

WordWright.biz, Inc.
WordWright Business Park
46561 State Highway 118
Alpine, TX 79830

Printed in the United States of America

All rights reserved. No part of this book may be reproduced or transmitted in any form by any means, electrical or mechanical, including photography, recording, or by any information or retrieval system without written permission of the author, except for the inclusion of brief quotations in reviews.

Library
University of Texas
at San Antonio

*To Brenda, Carole, Cynthia, Lynn,
and especially to Mary Jane, I miss you.*

Chapter 1

I woke with a start as our minivan plunged into a grove of giant old trees. The sun disappeared and a dark green tunnel enveloped us. Branches above us reached out to entwine their tips across the road. No sunlight penetrated their ancient arms, just a weird glow. I shivered and peered hard on either side of the road into thick brush.

"Is this Whitner?" I asked my father, who drove the minivan.

"We're on the edge, Josie. We should see houses any time now."

Then Dad eased the car around a curve, and the sun returned, filtered through big oaks. The trees still stretched tall, but they grew thinner here, and back from the road. I released the breath I didn't realize I'd held and inhaled deeply. I tried to shake off the strange feeling I'd gotten from the tree-tunnel.

"Was that stand of trees strange, or a dream?" Grandma sat, wide-eyed, next to Dad. "Are we in Whitner?"

"That scared me." My little brother, Ron sat tall in his seat now. "Neat, huh?"

I wasn't the only one with eerie feelings. What next, I wondered. Maybe an interesting summer?

Our summer plans included living in this old company town while Dad researched his book. We looked forward to a whole house to ourselves this year.

I could see the fallen chimney of a house off the left side of the road through the trees. Earlier, I saw vacant spaces where I expected to see houses. The words "house cemetery" popped into my head. Stop that, I told myself. This was just an old town.

"Dad," I said, leaning up toward the front seat, "Does anybody still live here?"

"No, everybody deserted it a long time ago." Sometimes people still lived in the company towns we visited for Dad's research, though most of the companies shut down years before.

"I've done some preliminary research on Whitner. Everyone left here long ago, and few people visit," he said, slipping into his professor mode. Dad worked on the history of company towns with a grant through the University of Alabama, where he taught.

"Grandma, Ron's bouncing again." I groaned, but still felt relief for the feel of the distraction. The whole back seat jostled. My little brother moved endlessly unless asleep. Something to do with red hair and freckles maybe.

"Ronnie, I know you're excited. We all are, but we're almost at the house. Please, try to sit still a little longer," Grandma said. I don't know how she kept her patience.

"There's our house," Dad said gesturing. He drove

around a circular driveway. Gravel crunched under the tires.

"Wow! That's a big old house," Ron shouted. He jumped from the car as soon as it stopped, then came back to Dad's window. "Hey, this house looks good. You said most of the houses here were falling down."

Dad got out, stretched his arms and rubbed his hand over his short sandy hair. "The house belongs to the Whitner family. They lived here during the steel mill's heyday. A caretaker visits occasionally to keep the place in good repair. It's in better shape than most of the houses. Look." He pointed. "See that one down the street?"

Ron swiveled to look at a house among the trees. "Yeah, there's big holes in that one. I'm glad we don't have to sleep there." That settled, he turned and ran toward the big house.

Grandma looked back at me. "Well, Josie-Rosie, Ronnie likes the house. Want to go explore?" I hate it when she calls me my baby name.

"Yeah, Ron likes most everything," I grumbled. "Let's do look inside." Tall trees shaded the large white house. They beckoned us toward the house, a relief after the eerie road into Whitner.

Ron scrambled up the steep steps. "Be careful, Ronnie," Dad called. Grandma and I followed them up to the wide porch. Ron waited, holding the screen door open.

Dad pulled a big key out of his jeans pocket and opened the door. "Slow down, Buddy."

Ron shot into the house, too excited to pay

attention. I felt excited about the house, too, but I don't overdo the enthusiasm like Ron does.

The front hall felt cool compared to the summer heat outside, and the house smelled like lemons and old furniture. A wide stairway reached up toward a landing. Sun gleamed on the shiny wood floor of the entry from the small window on the landing. This wasn't our little brick house at home in Tuscaloosa, for sure.

Ron bolted out of the kitchen, "Look in here, back stairs! And there's hiding places, Dad! Lots!" He tugged on Dad's hand to show what he'd found.

Grandma chuckled at them, then turned to me. "I'm going to see the kitchen, Josie. Want to come?"

"Maybe later, Grandma. I think I'll look upstairs first."

I climbed the big front stairs. I wanted to see my room. The stairs ended in a wide hall. Dad assigned me the first room on the right.

The room wasn't very big, but beneath four tall windows I saw a cushioned seat, its faded canvas cover formerly dark blue. Wide shelves stretched along one wall of the comfortable room. As I sat on the window seat to look out, my hand fell on something beside me on the cushion. A book.

The old book had a faded cover. I picked it up, *Little Women.* I remembered that book. I hugged it close. My mother had read it to me years ago not long before she died. When I opened the book, I could make out faded words inside the cover. I held the book close to the window and read.

Ag, I hope you love this book as much as I do, Love, Mother. May 13, 1937.

I wondered who left the book on the window seat, and who was Ag? 1937? Had she loved *Little Women* as much as her mother had? Probably. My mother and I loved that book. Had Ag's mother lived to see her grow up?

I looked out the window at the front yard of the house and the tall trees. As the sun went down, I saw a long shadow move out beyond the trees on the road. It looked like a girl, a tall, dark girl. She lifted her hand in a wave. I lifted mine, then I leaned closer to the window. I saw no one. Dad said nobody lived here. I'd find out about the girl when I started exploring the town tomorrow.

As I stared out at the gathering twilight, I felt a slight chill of expectation. Something was going to happen here. I knew it.

Chapter 2

By lunchtime the next day, my room looked as neat as I could make it. I set up my books in the bookcase and put my clothes away in the built-in drawers I found under the window seat. My computer sat on the desk in the corner of the room, hooked up and ready to go.

At noon, the family sat down to grilled cheese sandwiches and tomato soup at the small white wood table in the kitchen.

Dad looked at me. "You going to start your job today, Josie?"

I nodded. "Going to start soon, after lunch maybe."

"Good," he said.

Dad hired me to explore deserted Whitner, a job I'd do anyway. But he told me to see the town for him as his eyes. He mapped out Kessler, a small town about ten miles away, as his research site. The library there housed the Whitner papers.

I planned to look for the girl I thought I saw outside the house last night. I didn't mention her to Dad. I'd tell him if I found her.

Grandma looked at Dad. "Are you sure this town's safe for her to explore alone, Arthur?"

"The caretaker said no one lives here, Mom." He turned back to me. "Just take care around the old houses like we said, Josie. They might fall down around you. And don't go too far from here until I can go with you."

"Okay, Dad." I saw no worry in him, but Grandma needed no encouragement to fret.

"My meeting in Kessler should end before four. We'll meet you back here then," he said.

Grandma looked at Ron. "Ronnie's going to help me shop for groceries. Right, Sweetie?"

Ron grinned. "I'm a good helper."

"You can come with us, you know, Josie," Grandma said.

"No, thanks very much." She knew I hated shopping. Good that Ron liked going. Besides, I spent a lot of time alone and liked it, at least most of the time.

After they left, I went out through the backyard, past big bushes of bridal wreath and pink bushes of something good-smelling. Then I started down the hill toward the main part of the old community, where the workers lived. Dad said only the managers of the steel plant lived up here on the hill.

As the road curved downhill, the asphalt crumbled in places, and I watched my step to keep from stumbling. A small yellow house clung to the rocky edge of the road where the curve began to straighten.

And then I saw the girl again. She stood on the

steps of the little house below a faded sign: *Post Office, Whitner, Alabama.*

"Hey, how are you? I'm Lucy." African American, she looked my age, eleven, but stood taller. Her tight black curls shone in the sun. Her faded red dress hit her a little too far above the knees, small even for her bony frame.

I started up the steps toward the girl. "Hi, I'm Josie. I saw you yesterday afternoon waving at me."

"Yeah, that was me alright. You going to the town here?" She eased down to sit on the top step of the building.

"Yeah, my dad asked me to look at the place for him. Do many people come to see Whitner?"

"Not any more." She motioned her head toward the door of the building. "This here was the town post office. Everybody come here to get the mail."

I wondered if she'd show me the town.

"Doesn't look like we'll mail any letters there today." I peered in at a bare room through the dusty window of the door.

She laughed. "No, not hardly. Post office been closed a long time ago." She tucked the skirt of her faded red dress around her knees.

I sat down by her on the step. "My dad says nobody lives here any more. Do you live in Whitner?" I'd surprise him when I told him someone still lived here.

"Ain't supposed to be here, but I am. Don't tell nobody." She leaned toward me a little. "Might cause trouble if you do."

I didn't want to cause her family trouble. I could find out more about them. Then, if I needed to, I'd tell Dad. Besides, she seemed interesting, different. I wanted to get to know her. "Then I won't tell." I looked down the road past the post office. "Have you lived here long? Do you know anything about the town?"

She nodded. "Sure do. I been here a real long time. I know 'bout everything there is to know 'bout this town."

"Will you show me around?"

"Come on." She jumped up. "Know just where we can start out."

As we walked down the hill, I could see broken asphalt and worn gravel. We passed big yards with plants and flowers growing wildly over barely visible paths leading to places where houses once sat. The sun burned bright; no cemeteries here.

Down the road I saw a run-down house with an enormous old oak in front shading a weed-covered yard.

"Is that where you live, Lucy?"

"Naw. That's the old Ford place. Ain't many houses like this left to see. Most fell down long time ago." Lucy's teeth showed in a such a wide grin that I smiled back.

"Come on," she called as she loped toward the yard.

"Is this all right, to go here, I mean?" I followed her toward the house. "Is the house safe?" The wide front porch sagged in the middle, and the rusted screen

9

door hung open.

Lucy laughed as she stepped onto the porch. "Sure. Nothing and nobody here to bother us. This house a good one to see 'cause it's like most of the white folks' houses around here long time ago." The door creaked a little on its hinges as she opened it and went in. "Don't worry. Old man Ford treated people nice. This here's a good, friendly house."

The small house felt good somehow. Homey, even with the dust and without furniture. The rooms smelled faintly of cinnamon. It didn't match what I thought about old houses.

Lucy chatted and laughed as we ambled through the rooms. "Mr. and Miz Ford had a bunch of children." She told me funny stories about the family members as she pointed out the use for each room. I laughed with her at the stories.

"Did your grandma tell you all this? They left a long time ago, didn't they, the Fords?" We stepped into the old kitchen. Linoleum, cracked and worn thin, covered the floor, the color scrubbed away even before the dust covered it.

Lucy paid no attention to my question. She just laughed and went on talking. "Had biscuits ever meal, them Fords did. Made 'em right there." She pointed to an empty corner. "Table sat over on that side. Mr. Ford sat at the top, Miz at the bottom."

I could see the Ford family gathered at a big table in the corner. I knew all about the Fords, their children. and grandchildren by the time we came out of the house. Lucy's words made them come alive.

We headed back up the road the way we'd come with Lucy still giving out information. "All the men in this here town worked at the Whitner Iron Company making the steel, and the women, they shopped at the Whitner Commissary. Whitner family owned everything 'round here, houses and all, the people too, I reckon."

Lucy stopped walking when we got back to the post office. She looked off toward the woods across the road.

"Can we go inside the post office?" I glanced at the dusty windows of the little house.

"Not much in there, but tomorrow be best anyhow." She grinned. "Tomorrow, right here?"

I turned around and looked up at the sky behind us. I didn't need to go home yet. "We have some time." But no Lucy anywhere. "Good-bye," I called. She didn't answer. I started up the hill toward the house, but I looked back every now and then to see if I could spot her. No, she'd disappeared. I liked Lucy, felt like I had known her a long time. Unusual for me, especially with people my age. I smiled, thinking about the Ford house and the people who lived there. I wondered if she might have made the stories up.

That night at dinner, the family sat in the big kitchen around the small wooden table. We never sat in the big formal dining room with its enormous table that summer. The kitchen seemed much more friendly.

"James Whitner, the son of the company owner, grew up here in this house." Dad picked up his knife and fork to start on a pork chop as he told us about his day. "The family left here when James reached his teens. He's an old man now. But I think he could help me with details about the company. I'll start with the company records tomorrow at the Kessler Library." I knew he'd spend hours with those dusty old records. "Tell us what you saw today, Josie"

"You're careful, aren't you, sweetie?" Grandma took a small bite of mashed potatoes.

"Yes, ma'am. I won't go anywhere dangerous."

Ron stuffed his mouth and listened silently. He looked from one to the other as we spoke.

"I walked down the hill and looked in an old house, but I paid attention, Grandma. I made sure it was safe first." My grandmother looked doubtful. "I'll get all the details in my journal on the computer like you said, Dad. I'll print the information out for you when you're ready."

I wanted to tell them about Lucy and the Ford family. But I promised. I bit my lip to keep from telling about Lucy. I never wanted to tell about anyone as much as her. She made me laugh. I don't laugh very easily, not since Mom died, I guess.

After dinner, Ron tried out the new remote control car he got at the grocery store, his reward for helping Grandma shop. I went upstairs. I wanted to get started rereading *Little Women* anyway.

I sat at the computer for a while and wrote as much as I could about what I had seen that day. After I shut down, I put on my pajamas and went to retrieve *Little Women* from the window seat. The book was gone.

Chapter 3

"Josie, I do not know where to find your book," Ron said the next morning when I asked if he'd seen it. "Do you think I'd take your old book?" His lower lip stuck out.

Of course he hadn't taken the book. I couldn't picture what he'd want with it. Ron irritates me sometimes, like any seven-year-old, but he's really a pretty good kid.

But the book's whereabouts puzzled me. I'd torn up my room looking. Grandma and Dad hadn't seen the book.

If I wanted to go meet Lucy I'd have to forget about *Little Women* for now. I'd find it eventually.

"Grandma, there's so much to see in Whitner. Do you mind if I take a couple of sandwiches and have a picnic at lunchtime?" I wanted more time with Lucy.

"You're really enjoying your job, aren't you, Josie? Sure, have your picnic. Stay outside. That's good for you. I bet you'll find many nice old trees to sit under for a picnic. Enjoy yourself." I appreciated my grandmother. "But get home in plenty of time for dinner, please," she added. I appreciated her most of the time.

I fixed a couple of peanut butter and jelly sandwiches and put them in grocery bag with a couple of juice packs. Then I went down the hill to meet my new friend.

"Hey, where you been?" Lucy stood in the shade by the open door of the post office, wearing the same faded red dress as yesterday. "Don't matter, come on in."

The post office windows looked gray with dirt, but the sun shone brightly enough to let me see pretty well. Lucy pointed. "See them holes? That's where the man put the mail. Families sent somebody down here to get the mail ever day. Lots of times, the kids was the ones come."

"How long ago?" I'd like getting the mail first. I tried to imagine walking down the hill from the big house to the post office with all of the houses here.

"Post office been closed long time ago, real long time." I wondered how Lucy and her family got mail. Dad got us a post box in Kessler. Maybe they had one there.

"How 'bout I show you the old schoolhouse today?" We walked down the post office steps. "School been closed longer ago than the steel mill even, but lots of stuff got left in there."

"Sure," I said. "My dad wants me to see everything I can, as long as it's safe."

Lucy steered me down the street the way we'd gone the day before.

To get to the school, we passed the Ford place and

the field beside it where, Lucy said, Mr. Ford grew peanuts. The road turned into dust after that.

We climbed a hill. The summer air felt warm and smelled of green growing things. I smelled something slightly metallic. "Lucy, what's that smell?"

"Slag heap. Whitner always smell like that." She pulled at one of the weeds beside the path.

"What's a slag heap?" I looked back toward the dark form of the steel plant behind us in the distance.

"Slag what's left when they make the steel. Dumped it out in big piles after the furnace cooled off. Slag ain't there no more, but you still smell it. You get used to it."

I pulled in a deep breath. Mixed with the smell of growing things and the warm dust from the road, the odor wasn't bad. Somehow it suited the old town.

At the top of the hill, the road grew into a narrow path that curved between tall pine trees. The path led us to a weathered gray building about twice the size of the post office. Weeds grew up tall all around. The door swung in without a sound.

Inside, the sun broke through one large dusty window. I saw four rows of old fashioned desks. Bolts held each fast to the floor and to each other. A raised platform stood in front of the desks. On the wall, behind the platform hung a broken blackboard. Dust covered the desks and the floor.

I walked up one dusty row. "Why'd they leave the desks, Lucy?"

"Place closed up quick. Boss's daughter, she die. Boss Whitner, he shut the school down along with most everything else in town. Pretty soon, he shut the plant down. Then everybody left. Didn't take much with them from the schoolhouse, I reckon." Lucy stood by the door. She looked around the room searchingly.

I could almost see children sitting at the desks looking sad because they had to leave their school. I'd hate to change schools so suddenly.

"Did all the kids from Whitner come here?"

"White folks kids. Not the ones like me." She peered into the dark corners of the room.

I felt sadness in the room, then felt ridiculous.

"Bad news when the school closed." Lucy seemed sure of that. "You can tell how bad them children felt, can't you?"

I stared at the tall girl. Weird. She felt it, too.

"Ain't always like this here. Telling you somethin' maybe. Don't know."

"What do you mean? Who's telling me, and what?" The hair on the back of my neck prickled. What did Lucy know that I didn't?

"Not yet. Know soon, I reckon." Then she laughed at herself and took my hand. "Come on, show you happy stuff now."

Feeling hungry, I stopped Lucy at the Ford place. We flattened the weeds and sat in the shade of the old oak in the Ford's yard, so we could eat lunch. I tried to give Lucy one of the PBJ's, but she said she wasn't hungry. Without thinking, I ate both sandwiches as we talked and polished off the juice.

"What your school like, Josie? Not like Whitner's, I bet." She picked at the weeds beside us.

"No, my school's lots bigger." I chewed on a crust of bread "What's yours like?"

"You like to read books? What else you like to do at school?"

Okay, she didn't want to talk about her school. Maybe she doesn't go, I thought. I told her about the modern computer lab in our school, the principal's pride and joy. "I like to work with the computers."

"Computers, huh? Maybe I heard about them things some place." She slowly shook her head. "What 'bout you friends? They like them computer things?"

"Everybody likes the computers. Well, almost everybody. But I don't have many friends." I didn't think about it much any more, but I didn't hang out with anyone, even though I liked some of the girls in my class.

"Uh-huh." Lucy nodded. The way she said it made me think she understood.

"I guess living way out here it's hard for you to have many friends either. Do you have friends come to visit you and your family?"

Lucy got up. "Time we was going. Got more to show you. Good stuff, remember."

Lucy neatly avoided another question. Well, some people don't like to talk about their families. I stuffed the bag from lunch into the pocket of my shorts.

I got up and followed her back up the road.

The two of us spent the afternoon walking the paths in the woods across the street from the post office. Earlier, I saw all the trees across from the little building, but I didn't see a path until Lucy started down.

The refreshing cool of the woods brought out the birds, singing loudly. The place smelled fresh and untouched. We talked and talked like old friends. I felt like I could say anything to Lucy. We laughed at just about everything.

We stopped when we came to a large clearing in the wood. In the middle sat six or seven old, falling-down shacks. These tiny houses had never seen a can of paint. I think they had dirt floors.

"This where folks like me lived." She smiled as she looked around the clearing. "Lots of love down here. Folks live down here had lots of fun times. Had get-togethers all time. Oo–ooo, the food they gave us! Good times here."

"Were the people who lived down here poor?" I wondered how people could be happy and live in those shacks.

"Everybody poor back then. Didn't matter much. Had gardens, chickens, pigs. Nobody hungry here." She looked off into the woods.

I tried again to find out more. "Lucy, how do you know all these things about Whitner?" But she seemed lost in thought. "Just do. You best go on home now." She spoke absently. "Come on, I take you out to the road."

I agreed. We'd spent the day exploring and I felt tired. I knew not to be late for dinner, not to worry Grandma.

Lucy followed behind me on the path, singing a song I knew, and I joined in.

Do Lord, oh do Lord, Oh, do remember me!
Do Lord, oh do Lord, Oh, do remember me!

"With these voices, they'd never pick us for the church choir," I remarked.

"Yeah, you right, but we good and loud, ain't we?" That got us laughing again.

As I stepped off the path and onto the road, I remembered all the things I had forgotten to ask Lucy. I turned around. "Where does your family live, Lucy? Can I call you? I'm not sure when I can come back."

She'd vanished again.

"Lucy?" I called. How did she do that? I thought as I walked up the hill toward home. She disappears without a sound? Ron sneaked up silently. He and Lucy should get together.

Dad began to talk as soon as we sat down to dinner that night. "I found most of the Whitner Company history in the library." He waved his hands around the way he did when he got excited about a project. "I brought home a book, *Whitner Iron Company, Alabama Blast Furnaces*. The author wrote it long before the place closed."

"Is the information interesting this time, Arthur?" Grandma often asked him that when he started researching one of his old company towns every summer.

"Well, I found something that makes this town different from others I've studied, Mom." I looked up. I thought this town different myself.

Dad went on as he picked at his dinner. "I'm just beginning, of course, but I can't understand why the town died so quickly after the steel plant closed. The people left even though they didn't need to. A few of them might live here even now, if they lasted long enough. I have to look much more carefully at the material to find out what happened. I'm going to get an early start in the morning."

Silently, I agreed. I thought Whitner very unusual. I might even call it mysterious.

I thought about the feeling I'd had in the schoolhouse. As much as I enjoyed Lucy, I didn't understand her disappearing act. Lucy knew so much about this town, though she wouldn't say how she knew. I'll bet she knew why everybody left when the plant closed. I wondered if she'd tell me.

When I went upstairs to read later, I had to start a new book. I still hadn't found the copy of *Little Women.*

Chapter 4

Dad left so early the next morning that I didn't hear him go. At breakfast, Grandma told me she needed my help. "Can you watch Ronnie for me this morning, Josie, keep him busy?"

"I planned on going down the hill again, Grandma, but, I guess, if you need me." I couldn't tell her about meeting Lucy.

Grandma grinned. "Just keep him busy for a couple of hours. I need to touch up my hair and do my nails. I've let myself go since we arrived. You can go exploring after."

"Okay, sure, Grandma, but I think you look good now." What else could I do? She hardly ever asked, and I knew she needed time to herself. I found Ron out back throwing his baseball into the air and catching it. He looked so natural. Even with two more hands, I'd miss the ball.

"Want to play catch?" I could do that, if we stood close.

Ron smiled and threw me the ball, which I promptly missed. He patiently tossed it, back and forth, not saying anything when I missed his throws.

"What's down the hill, Josie?" He tossed the ball.

"Not much, Ron." I reached out and actually caught it. I tossed the ball back.

He held the ball and studied it carefully. "I bet ghosts live in those houses."

"Oh Ron, there's no such thing as ghosts. You know that." He loved ghost stories. Grandma usually gave in and read them to him. She could tell them, too. Sometimes I even liked them.

"Bet ghosts *do* live there," he said. He came closer to me. "Will you tell me if you see any? I'd sure like to see a ghost."

"Ron, if I see a ghost, I'll certainly let you know." I laughed.

"Promise?" His freckled face looked solemn.

I raised my right hand. "I promise."

He looked cute when he got so serious. At least he didn't ask if he could go exploring with me, not yet. I told him to get his bat and I'd pitch him some balls for practice. He hit quite a few, and I chased after them. I think he took it easy on me though.

Grandma called us for lunch just as I chased after a ball.

I wolfed down my bologna and pickle sandwich and gulped the milk.

"Thank you, Josie, for the help." Grandma winked. "I'm all done. You can go do your exploring now."

As I went out the kitchen door, Ron yelled, "Don't forget!"

I grinned at him.

I found Lucy on the post office steps. "I'm really sorry, Lucy. I had to baby-sit my little brother this morning."

"Don't matter. Got nothing but time." She got up slowly without a smile.

I tried to think of something funny to say to cheer her up, but I'm not good at thinking up funny stuff. So I asked her where we'd go.

"First, maybe, the old commissary. That's where everybody bought the food, clothes and everything. That okay?"

"Sure, I told you, I want to see everything."

"You goin' to see it all." She chuckled and this made me feel better.

We went down the hill, then turned in the opposite direction from the Ford house. Along the gravel road, we passed several old houses. Some of them had fallen in on themselves, roofs collapsed. One leaned to the side as if it in danger of any wind. Dying houses. They made me sad.

Then we walked past a flat field filled with tall yellow-topped weeds. On the other side of the field I saw the old plant, a big brick building. It loomed close. Three stories of little windows, some of them broken, faced the field. I spied the tall chimneys of the furnaces behind the building and smelled the strong odor of slag.

"Was noisy down here in the old days. They fired up them furnaces to make the steel...sounded like a big ol' giant hissing snake. 'Course you could hear the noise all over town, but real big right here."

I didn't even bother to ask Lucy how she knew. I enjoyed the mystery, at least for a while longer.

A barn-like brick building, the commissary smelled moldy and sour. Trash littered the place and pipes stuck out of the walls.

"Not much left here, huh?" I wondered why we'd come here. "What about the plant? Do you ever go there?" I asked. "Anything there to see?"

"Naw. They got somebody there watch the place and keep out folks. Don't know why."

I didn't care. The plant looked forbidding somehow.

"Could go see the infirmary, if you want to." She said this slowly. "Right back yonder." She pointed toward a small door.

"What's an infirmary?" I asked. The dust stirred and made me sneeze as we walked across the room.

"Where the sick folks went, sick white folks anyway." She walked ahead of me toward the door. "Stuff still there like at the school. Closed up 'bout the same time."

"Sure, let's go. You're in charge."

She laughed loud. "Got that right!"

We went through the small door at the rear of the commissary, down the cement steps of a loading dock, to a path along the back. I spotted a faded white building a short way down a red dirt road running along the side of the commissary.

The wood-shingled infirmary building was larger than both the post office or the school, its small, evenly spaced windows crusted with dust. A weedy path, still lined with stones, led to the front door. Some kind of large leafed trees grew tall behind and shaded the building.

Lucy slowed as we neared the steps leading up to a small porch. "This place different from the others, Josie. You need to watch youself here."

"Are there holes in the floor?" Lucy's unusual warning threw me. "I'll take care where I step, okay?"

"No holes in the floor, but you need to watch yourself, you hear?" Her voice sounded strange, raspy. She opened the door and motioned me in.

Inside, only dim light filtered through the dirty windows. The air felt chilly, but thick. I stood near the door while my eyes adjusted to the darkness. Sadness seemed to swallow me up. I thought maybe I had started to cry. Then I realized that the crying didn't come from me, but from somewhere in the building.

"Lucy?" I called, but Lucy didn't answer. I stumbled farther into the room. My foot hit something and I almost fell. I reached down and picked up a book. I'd stumbled over a book. I held on to it.

The crying grew louder. Someone sobbed. Not Lucy. The voice sounded younger. I looked all around the room. Two old rusting metal beds, no mattresses, no young girl. I floundered on through the room to an open door in the back. I searched for a little girl, the source of the voice I heard.

The crying stopped when I stepped through a doorway into a small room. My sadness went away; strong anger replaced it. I staggered back as if I'd run into a wall. Something grabbed my hand and I cried out.

"Me, Josie. Just me." What a relief to hear Lucy's voice. "Come on. Come on." She pulled me from the infirmary quickly and closed the door.

For a few minutes, I just stood there taking deep breaths, staring at the closed door. "Lucy, what happened in there? Did you hear that little girl crying? Did you see her?"

"She be fine soon, I think. Sorry. Just couldn't tell you. You all right now, ain't you?" She looked at me closely, then she grinned. "Thought you was the one."

What one? I trembled and I wanted to get away from there. "Lucy, show me how to get back to the post office, right now." I felt angry. If she knew about the infirmary, why did she let me go in there?

"Come on. I tell you all about everything. Don't be mad at me."

I followed her down the road. I realized I still held the book I'd picked up in the infirmary. I stopped walking and looked at it. *Little Women*. I flipped open the cover.

Ag, I hope you love this book as much as I do,
Love, Mother.
May 13, 1937.

I stood still staring at the page. How could my book have gotten in the infirmary?

"Come on, Josie. We almost back."

Lucy's voice brought me back to the road, and we walked on. My mind scrambled, trying to comprehend how the book got on the floor of the infirmary. I couldn't think anymore. We got back to the post office and I flopped on the steps. My legs wouldn't hold me up any more. I looked up at Lucy. "What?" I said, willing her to talk.

"Yeah, you want to know everything. Can you wait 'til tomorrow? Getting awful late." Lucy seemed so solemn and certain. "Everything be okay. You be all right."

"No, you tell me now. I need to know now."

I could still hear the crying child in my mind.

"You read you book, you hear? I got to go," Lucy said firmly.

I looked down at my feet. I felt so tired. I saw no Lucy when I looked up. No surprise there. I wondered how to get that poor crying child out of my mind. My eyes wandered to the book in my hand. I opened it and began to read *Little Women*.

"Christmas won't be Christmas without any presents," grumbled Jo, lying on the rug.

"It's so dreadful to be poor!" sighed Meg, looking down at her old dress.

After reading for a while, I felt a little better. My mother and I read these familiar words together. As I read, her comforting arm wrapped around my shoulder, as if she sat beside me. I didn't want to stop. But the afternoon shadows grew long, so I pulled myself up from the steps and went home.

I pretended I felt fine, but I couldn't eat much at dinner because my stomach churned.

"You need to eat, Josie Rosie." Grandma sounded

concerned. "Something wrong?"

"No, I'm fine." I forced a smile. Grandma knew me too well. I moved the food around on my plate, making holes to look like missing bites.

Dad chattered about new information he discovered, more talkative than I'd heard him since last summer.

"Old Mr. Whitner's daughter died at only eight years old. Shortly after she died the plant closed. They had a teenage boy, too. They all lived right here back in the thirties, you know." He put down his fork. "Mom, they had servants taking care of this big house then. Too bad we can't afford servants for you."

Grandma laughed. "We're only using a few rooms. No problem as long as you don't mind a little dust." She wrinkled her nose. "Do you think the death of Mr. Whitner's daughter somehow caused the plant to close, Arthur?"

"I'm trying to find out, Mother. I still have to interview the Whitner boy tomorrow. Well, he's not a boy, of course, but an old man in his seventies or eighties. Maybe he can tell me what happened back then. The plant definitely went downhill quickly after the girl's death. Maybe her father just lost his will to work the place after she died." He looked at me for a minute before turning back to Grandma.

"I'd like to interview some of the men and women who used to live in Whitner, or at least their children. So far I can't find any of them. I can't begin to guess why they all moved out."

Ron ate quietly until then. "Daddy, what made that

little girl die? Eight's almost the same age as me."

Grandma patted Ron's hand. "Oh, Ronnie, that happened a long time ago. Now they make good medicines, and if you get sick those medicines will make you well again."

"Absolutely, Ron," Dad nodded. Then he turned to Grandma. "I need to find out what killed her, though. Maybe the way she died caused a problem. If the Whitners can't tell me, maybe I can find the doctor from the infirmary and talk to him."

I wanted to tell Dad about Lucy because she likely knew. But I needed to hear her story first. So I kept Lucy to myself for now.

Then a thought hit me. "Did the girl die in this house, Dad?"

"No, Josie. From what I've read, I think she died in the Whitner Infirmary, a place like a hospital."

I wondered what her voice sounded like...the sobbing voice I'd heard in the infirmary. But how could a dead person cry?

My mind jolted into overload again, so I kept quiet. As soon as I could, I escaped upstairs to read *Little Women*. I read myself to sleep.

Chapter 5

I tossed and turned that night. I dreamed of a faceless, weeping child. Sometimes I saw her in the infirmary, sometimes in my room. I awoke myself bawling as the sun cast shadows through the big trees into my window. How foolish! I wiped my eyes with the edge of the sheet.

I missed everyone else, so I had cereal by myself at the kitchen table. Ron came in just as I rinsed the bowl at the sink.

"Well?" he said, lowering his voice. "Anything yet?"

"Huh?" I said. "Oh, ghosts. Yeah. I mean no. No ghosts, Ron." I wanted to tell somebody about the voice in the infirmary, and I considered telling Ron. He'd at least believe me. But I had to talk to Lucy before I told anybody anything. I needed to hear what Lucy had to say.

Ron waited in the doorway. He looked skeptical, as if he knew I held something back.

"Ron, I promise. No ghosts in Whitner so far." I crossed my heart with my finger and held up my hand. I didn't lie. I hadn't seen anything, but I'd started to wonder about ghosts.

"Yeah, okay, I guess." He sighed. "But you'll tell me if you do, 'cause you promised." With a wave of his hand, he went out the back door.

I went out the front.

I hurried down the hill to the post office. Lucy wasn't there yet. I sat on the steps and waited. I wondered about her absence. She always arrived first. Well, sometimes I got here late. I sat for a while, waiting, thinking about what Lucy might tell me. I'd like the truth.

Time moved on, and still no Lucy. Anger and worry fought with each other inside my head. I got up and paced in front of the post office. I should go look for her, I thought. If she came here, she'd wait like she always did.

Still, I waited 'til I couldn't stand waiting any more. Then I set out to look for her.

I looked at the Ford house first, calling out Lucy's name along the way. She wasn't there, or at the school, or down the path across from the post office. I knew I wasn't going to the infirmary if I could help it. Maybe I'd find her at the commissary. I called for her every few minutes.

At the field near the old plant, my voice echoed eerily, "Lucy...ucy...ucy." I shivered in spite of the hot summer sun. How goofy. When I neared the big store, I heard something. Maybe a cat, I thought. I heard it again, far away and small, "Josie!" Someone called my name this time.

I answered, "Lucy? That you?"

"Josie!" A little louder now.

I recognized Lucy's voice. It came from the direction of the infirmary. No. I didn't want to go back there. "Lucy, come here now," I shouted.

"Josie!" She sounded upset. I edged past the commissary toward the white building down the dirt road. I'd go just a little closer.

"Come on, Josie!" The upset voice, Lucy's called from inside the infirmary. I knew what to do. I forced myself to take firm strides to the infirmary and up the steps. I hesitated for a few seconds, then I turned the knob and leaned in the doorway calling.

"Lucy? You in here?" I heard rustling inside. I forced my legs to step into the dimness. The door slammed shut behind me. For several moments I saw nothing. Then I saw a different room from the day before. Mattresses and linens covered the two beds. Through the murky light, I could see someone on one of them. "Lucy, what's going on?"

A young girl sat up slowly in the bed. Her face looked small and pale. Her long, blond hair and high-necked gown seemed to glow in the darkness. "Who...," I stammered. The little girl began to cry. Big sobs shook her. I ran to her without thinking, but as I got to the bed, she faded from view. Before me sat nothing but a rusty old bed frame.

I think my heart stopped beating. I sensed something behind me and whirled around to look. A man stood in the doorway of the little back room. My heart started to beat again, a fierce pounding in my chest. The man's large potbelly bulged, covered by a dingy, colorless shirt that hung over shapeless tan trousers. His bald head shone. White hair frizzled out behind large wrinkled ears. He grinned, but not a good grin. I froze, staring. Then he, too, faded away to nothing.

"Josie, can't you hear me calling you?"

Lucy. I numbly looked toward the front door. She leaned in and motioned to me to come out. I ran to her. She pulled me through the door.

She looked at me. "You had to go back in that place again, I reckon."

"I went in looking for you. I heard your voice. You sounded hurt." The words came out in a rush. "Where did you go?" My anger returned now that I realized Lucy was safe.

"Looking for you!" She frowned. "I found you, didn't I?"

"Yeah, I guess." Relief washed over me; I didn't want to argue.

"Guess you saw them. Guess they wanted you to see them." My head jerked up. "You've seen them ?"

"Yeah, for long, long time."

"Do you know them?"

"For so long you ain't going to believe me." She looked over my shoulder at the white building.

"The little crying girl, I heard her yesterday. The boss's daughter?"

Lucy stared at me. "How you know that?"

I told her about my father's research and his plans to interview the Whitners today.

"Are you going to tell me about them now?" I spat

out the words. I'd had more than enough mystery. I wanted the truth.

Lucy took a deep breath. "Not here. Come on."

"Okay, but you stay with me until I know what's going on."

I refused to let her disappear again. I grabbed her hand and told myself I'd hold it until I had the truth.

Instead of stopping at the post office as usual, Lucy led me down the path across the street. The sun shone through the tall trees making leafy patterns on the ground. Birds sang. Insects buzzed. Very normal and ordinary.

The story that Lucy told me was anything but ordinary.

Chapter 6

"Aggie, Aggie Whitner. That the little girl you seen." Lucy began her story as we settled on the mossy ground under a large oak tree. I leaned forward, intent on listening.

"Best I start back at the first." She tucked her red dress under her legs. "Aggie live in that house you living in now, long time ago. Me and her became friends."

"You mean Aggie talks to you?"

"No, Josie. Way back then, we made friends. She only eight, but her and me we liked each other. We meet right outside her yard in back most ever day."

I shook my head. "But, Lucy, the girl died so long ago. I don't understand."

"You think about it, you understand all right."

So Lucy lived when Aggie Whitner did? Lucy a ghost? I could think of no other explanation. The truth stood right in front of me all along. The way Lucy disappeared without a sound. She wouldn't tell me where she lived. But most of all, she knew all about the past, details she could only know if she'd lived then. Still, she seemed so real!

"Now you listen to what I say, then you ask all you questions, all right?" Lucy went on with the story. "Aggie, she let me hold her pretty baby dolls. She even teach me 'bout reading and stuff after she started going to school. She little, but she a good friend, like you."

I liked the way Lucy called me her good friend. And I knew I'd stay her friend no matter what she told me.

Lucy looked down at the moss beneath us, smoothing it with the palm of her hand. "On this one day, Aggie, she didn't come to meet me. That happen sometime. I think, she just busy with her mama. She be back tomorrow. Three, four days go by and I got 'fraid.

"Next day, I ease up to the back door of the big house where I'm not supposed to go. Cook, she see me and say, 'Girl, what you doing here?' I say, 'You seen Aggie?' Cook say, 'Poor little thing. She sick bad. Boss, he take her to that infirmary.'

"I got away from that house 'fore Boss seen me. I run to the infirmary. Had to sneak up to one of them windows. I peek in. I saw Aggie in a bed looking almost white as that sheet that cover her. Nobody else in the room with her, so I knock a little on the window. Aggie, she look at me and she smile, real weak, but a smile." Lucy cleared her throat.

"Then old Dr. Percy, he come in. I get away from there fast. I figure if Aggie could smile, she get well soon." Lucy stopped for a minute looking out through the trees.

She went on. "Doctor, when he come in, he held a

36

big bottle. Maybe medicine, maybe not. Sure looked like the bottle I seen my uncle drinking from right 'fore my mama throw him out of the house."

She stopped talking for a long time. She looked up at the big oak above us, then down to her hands clasped together in her lap.

I couldn't stand it any more. "Lucy, what happened?"

She looked at me like she'd forgotten I sat right beside her. Then she started again. "Aggie, she don't get okay. Next morning, everybody saying Boss Man's daughter died. Gonna be big, big trouble. Me, I run fast as I can to the infirmary, not believin' Aggie dead.

"When I get there, I go right to the door this time. I got to see little Aggie. They pulled that white sheet over Aggie's face. I know Aggie's dead.

"Boss Whitner and Jamie, Aggie's big brother, standing by the bed. The boy cried, but Boss look mad.

"Then Dr. Percy come out of the back, kinda' weaving 'round and staggering. Boss, he turn to the doc and start yelling bad words. Then he raise up that cane he always carry, the one with the gold on top, and he hit the doctor. Doc, he fall down on the floor, but Boss, he just keep hitting and hitting, till that doc, he not move. His head look bad.

"Then Boss turn around and he see me. He look at that boy. He put his hand on my shoulder, holdin' me hard. Then he say, 'Take you sister out of here. I take care of this pickaninny.' He mean me. That what he call us children. He make me go with him.

"I don't remember no more."

I stared at her, and I knew all of this really happened to her. She told the truth.

But she wasn't done with her story. "Later, I come back here to Whitner somehow. Nobody around down here where I lived, nobody. The houses, they empty. Boss Whitner done sent all of them away, I reckon, my momma and daddy too. I got no place to go.

"I go to Mr. Ford's place. My mama, she clean for the Fords long time. They always good to us. Maybe they know where all the folks has gone.

"Mr. Ford, he look at me and his eyes get wide. He just yell, 'No! Go 'way! You dead! I saw your body after they pull it out of the reservoir.' He look real scared.

"Then I remember about Boss hitting me and throwin' me in the reservoir." She paused. "I know what I am. Everybody know 'bout how I died, I reckon. Other folks see me sometime. They run away fast.

"Now you know 'bout me. You goin' to run?"

I looked at her. I didn't feel afraid of Lucy, my friend. Everything made sense now. "Are you really my friend like you said?" I covered her hand with mine.

"Course I am." She looked into my eyes. "What else you want to know?" She smiled and held my hand with both of hers.

"You're just like me. You're here and you're real." I patted her hand. "Is Aggie really here? Why can't I see her all the time?"

"I ain't sure. She here, but not. Kinda' part way

between here and the resting. That man you see?"

The thought of him made me shiver. "He's scary. I'd run from him for sure."

"He mad at Boss for what he did. He just mad at Boss. Aggie say she died 'cause she real sick. But the doc, he real drunk. Boss, he lose his little girl and kill the doc. Then he kill me."

"Why do Aggie and the doctor stay here? I'm glad I met you. But I don't understand why you're all still here." I stumbled over the words not knowing how to ask.

"You only one glad you met me, 'sides Aggie, I mean." Lucy went on thoughtfully. "I think I got it figured out, why we here. That doc, he so mad he killed like that. The feeling so strong, he can't get gone. Aggie, she here 'cause of the doc, 'cause her daddy kill the doc. She won't leave the man here by hisself. Guess maybe she can't leave him."

"Are you here because you're angry at Mr. Whitner?" I couldn't imagine that, although Whitner gave her a good reason.

"Me, I think I come to get Aggie. I love that little girl. She so unhappy here. I think I supposed to find a way to get her gone. I ain't found no way yet. I can't go 'less she go. I won't go 'less she go. I'm here because of the love. Maybe love stronger than hate, that why I'm more here than them, I reckon."

I sat for a few minutes thinking about her theory. Yes, Lucy had that much love in her. I'd always felt that. "Then I'll have to help you to help Aggie. We'll think of something we can do."

I hadn't known Lucy long, but I thought of her as my first real friend. Of course I had to help her, and I wanted to help poor little Aggie.

"You once said I was 'the one'." I stopped for a minute. "Did you mean I can do something to help?"

"Yeah. You the first one 'sides me ever able to see the doc and Aggie. When people lived here in Whitner, they see me and get scared. But nobody 'cept me see or hear Aggie and the doc 'fore you come. Some reason you see them."

Lucy smiled then looked around. "Getting late. You out here all day. Go now and think on it. Me, I'm gonna think a bunch."

"Are you sure you're going to show up tomorrow? I don't want to go back to the infirmary to find you again." I smiled as I said it. I knew we'd moved past all that disappearing stuff now.

"You come right here. I be here. We make plans, if you still want to help tomorrow." She got up and pulled me up with her.

"I'm going to help. We'll find a way." I squeezed her hand and turned to go down the path.

"Hey, Josie." I looked back at her. "Glad you come here. Glad you goin' to help us."

I smiled at her again, then walked down the path toward home. I just had to help. We'd find a way.

Chapter 7

Ghosts! Why didn't I shake with fear? Instead, I felt relief at the story Lucy told about death and murder. I knew the truth now.

I also felt relieved that I hadn't told my dad about Lucy. He believed me about most things. But he'd never believe I had seen ghosts. Even Grandma wouldn't believe the ghosts. Heck, I wouldn't believe me! But I saw them.

I had to concentrate on how I could help Lucy and her friend. We'd get no help from the grownups.

Grandma let me know of her disappointment in me when I got home so late. I'd missed lunch, too, without letting her know. She worried about me. I apologized and promised never ever to do it again before she quit lecturing me. Still, she didn't ground me, restrict me to the house for a week. I think she sensed that she shouldn't.

"How's your job coming, Josie?" Dad asked after we all sat down at the table. "Are you ready to show me around the town this weekend?"

"Sure." I wondered if I could dodge that. Or should I dodge it? "How's your research coming,

41

Dad?" I put my napkin in my lap. Let him talk while I had time to think.

"Yes, Arthur," Grandma chimed in as she put baked beans on Ron's plate, "I'd like to hear about your research. Did you learn anything more today? Did you talk to the Whitners?" She nibbled at her hot dog.

"I didn't learn much." Dad crunched a potato chip. "The Whitner son said he doesn't know why the people left Whitner when they weren't required to go."

Ron looked up from his hot dog. "I think ghosts took all the people." He sounded serious.

Dad and Grandma both laughed. I looked at Ron closely until he turned to look at me. Did he know something? He's a bright little boy.

"Maybe, Ronnie." Dad grinned at Ron. "But I kind of doubt it." He turned to Grandma. "Lots of ghost stories lately, Mom?"

"You know how he loves to hear them, Arthur." She turned to Ron. "Ronnie, I make up the ghost stories. They're pretend, not real. Remember, we talked about that?" Grandma smiled as she chewed.

"What did Mr. Whitner say, Dad?" He for sure didn't tell Dad what really happened.

Dad put his fork down. "James Whitner said that his family moved into Kessler after his little sister died. The family didn't want to stay in the house without her. Not long after she died, when the steel plant closed, all the families moved out of Whitner. Mr. Whitner didn't seem to care why."

Dad picked up his fork, but he didn't start eating again. "I keep trying to find someone else who lived here in Whitner back then. Mr. Whitner didn't know of anybody. If I could find someone, even someone who lived here as a child then, they might remember something to give me a clue about what happened."

Dad always wrote about the people in the company towns he studied. I'd heard another professor say the people stories made Dad's books on the history of company towns good. An awful lot of students crowd into his classes at the University.

"I still think ghosts made them leave." Ron wasn't backing down an inch, even if the grownups didn't take him seriously.

"I suppose that makes for an easy solution, son," Dad said. "I did find out something interesting at today's interview. Homer Whitner, James's father, is still alive. He's very old and doesn't want to talk to anyone, according to James."

"Well I never," said Grandma. "What's his age? Late nineties or maybe even a hundred, I'll bet. And probably not in good health, Arthur."

Dad sighed. "That's probably true, Mom. I'd like to talk to him, though. I doubt if his son will let me. He seems very protective."

"Maybe they're the ghosts." Ron mumbled just loud enough for me to hear. I fought a giggle.

I knew if I told Ron about the ghosts he'd believe me. You believe what your big sister says when you're only seven. I might have to get him to help me with Lucy, but I didn't want to not if I could find another way.

Lucy needed to know first thing that Boss Whitner

still lived. Boss caused everything that happened to the doctor and to Lucy. And to Aggie.

That night I saw Aggie in my room. Asleep for a while, I woke up not knowing why. I looked toward the window and the moonlight that drifted brightly into the room.

Aggie sat on the window seat holding *Little Women*, her long blond hair streaming down the back of her high-necked nightgown. I didn't feel afraid, maybe because I knew more about Aggie now.

In the morning, I thought about seeing Aggie and decided I dreamed it. I rushed over to the window seat as soon as the sun woke me. No book. So I hadn't dreamed Aggie. It made me feel good that she took the book. Maybe the book made her feel close to her mother. I remembered that she looked happy last night. She smiled at me and I smiled back. Then she slowly faded out of sight. The book faded with her.

Chapter 8

Lucy waited just as she promised. She smiled as I walked toward her. The birds in the tree above her sang to the morning.

"You know something new, don't you? Tell by the way you grinning." I sat down beside her. She turned to me and raised her eyebrows. "Well?"

I smiled. "I think the news will help us, but I want to see what you think." Then I told her what I'd learned from my father last night, about old Mr. Whitner still living in Kessler.

"Boss Whitner alive. Don't that beat all." She shivered slightly. "Might could help us some, I reckon."

Insects hummed all around. I slapped at a mosquito on my knee.

"Lucy, I saw Aggie in my room last night. On the window seat. And she smiled this time."

"You saw her in your room?" Lucy stretched her legs out on the smooth moss and leaned back on her elbows. "That room got lots of places you put books at?"

"Yes, and I like to read in the window seat. I bet

Aggie liked to, too. She took her book away with her."

"You staying in Aggie's room. She told me 'bout that room a hundred times. I loved to hear 'bout it. Guess she go there now sometime. Guess she get more places. I don't know. Felt like her in that schoolhouse. Didn't know for sure."

Lucy grinned as she sat up again. "She must know you trying to help. Aggie and me, we together, but not, you know? She know I see her. Now she know you see her."

I lifted Lucy's hand from her lap. "All this time you've been here. That's hard, I bet." I looked into her big brown eyes and saw sadness deep within. "I bet you get lonely, too."

"Just tired, I suppose. Want to go home. Want to rest. Maybe you and me, we fixing to get me and Aggie home." Lucy looked down at our hands clasped together.

She seemed so strong, but I knew she needed to move on and needed my help.

"Don't do no good feeling bad like that now." She sat up straight. "Now. What we gonna' do?"

"I thought about that. You say the doctor refuses to go because of his anger at Boss Whitner. What if we got the two of them together, got Mr. Whitner to come to the infirmary? Do you think that might help the doctor?" I pictured the doctor and shuddered. "Or do you think it's too dangerous?"

Lucy sat quietly for a few minutes. "Don't know. Might be scary, but...feels right, don't it? How we do that?"

"I think maybe there's a way. If Mr. Whitner can still get out of the house, if he can still walk around, maybe we can get him to the infirmary. If my dad finds out what I've done I'll probably get grounded for the rest of my life, but if the plan works...." I trailed off thinking about the plan that took shape in my mind.

"You gonna' tell me, Josie? Please." Lucy's eyes sparkled with excitement. I leaned forward to fill her in on my plan. Her grin grew larger as I talked.

"I must figure out exactly how to get the note to Mr. Whitner. The message has got to go right to him, not anybody else. That leaves out sending it by mail. I doubt he gets his own mail. I may have to get my little brother to help us."

"Your little brother tell you Daddy?"

"No, I don't think so. I'll tell Ron about the ghosts and swear him to secrecy. I know he won't tell for a while. Long enough, I hope." I felt sure Ron could keep the secret for a while, but not for long. I'd get in trouble later, a small thing if we accomplished this.

"You go on home then and get things started, Josie. Talk to your little brother."

"Yeah." I got slowly to my feet. "Can you tell Aggie we're trying to help her?"

"Going to take a crack at it. Never know for sure if she know what I say, but I try." Lucy got up. "Her smiling at you, I think maybe she already know."

We walked down the sun-dappled path silently. A bobwhite called from somewhere in the woods.

"Bob, bobwhite!" The bird's clear call seemed like a good sign.

Chapter 9

After lunch, I curled up in one of the old wicker chairs on the shady front porch and tried to think about how I could deal with the note and help Lucy and her little friend. I studied the huge trees in the front yard. For a while I thought only of how pleasant it seemed on the porch where the trees hid the outside world.

Finally, my mind snapped back to ideas for delivering the note. Could I deliver it without Ron's help? What could I do to get to Kessler?

If I said I wanted to go to the library for books, I'd hitch a ride with Dad. But then I'd have to stay with him in the library. He'd probably put me to work helping him with research, leaving me no way to escape and take the note to Boss Whitner.

Grandma went to Kessler for groceries, another option for me to hitch a ride. But then I'd have to spend all my time helping her. Again, no way to deliver the note. Besides, she knew I hated shopping, so she'd definitely watch me closely. I felt like she already suspected I was up to something.

Now, if Ron went, we'd figure out a way to escape the grownups. I took him to the library and sometimes to the movies in Tuscaloosa, and Kessler was a lot smaller. With no other options for delivering the note, I decided on taking Ron. I knew he'd want to help.

I promised to tell him about any ghosts. I found him behind the house. He squatted just inside the yard watching ants mill about their mound. "Better leave those fire ants alone, Ron. They bite."

"I know that. I'm careful." He looked annoyed.

"I know. In fact, I want you to help me with something important, something that requires great care."

"What do you want help with?" He brightened.

"It's about ghosts."

"Ghosts? What ghosts?" I'd hooked him. I led him around the house to the front porch. We sat together on the top step.

I told him about what I had seen in the infirmary. Then I told him the story Lucy had told me. His eyes got wider and wider.

"Is all that really true? Cross your heart?" He asked this with his solemn expression.

"Cross my heart and hope to die." I made a big X with my finger across my chest again.

He sat for a minute looking down at the steps. "What do you want me to do?"

"I want you to help me get to Kessler to deliver a note."

"What kind of note? Deliver it to who? Do I get to see the ghosts?" He jumped up and bounced from one foot to another.

"I'll take you down to meet Lucy if you want, if

you don't tell Grandma. You really don't want to see the others though, trust me."

I wasn't going to put the kid through that, or me either. The doctor's nasty smile came to mind. I didn't want Ron to have to see him.

Grandma seemed pleased that I wanted to take Ron with me on my exploring trip that afternoon. "Have a good time, kids. I'm glad you'll have company down there this afternoon, Josie." I knew she'd worried about me.

Ron and I went down the hill toward the post office. He ran in circles around me. Lucy wasn't there, but we found her. She had gone back down the path in the wood. She sat under the big oak tree in the shade.

I watched Ron for signs of fear, but after I introduced him, he said, "You're not a ghost. You're just a girl."

Lucy laughed out loud. "You right, little Ronnie. A girl. That me." She turned to me. "He 'bout Aggie's age, ain't he, Josie?"

Ron stretched himself up tall. "I'm seven years old."

I squatted down beside Ron and looked him in the eye. "You have to trust me, Ron. I told you all about Lucy. She's a ghost. She's also a good friend. We have to help her." I settled beside her under the tree.

Ron gazed hard at her. "Yeah, okay. If you say she's a ghost, she's a ghost." He poked Lucy's arm with a finger. "I just thought she'd look scarier." He sat down beside me. "What do I do to help her and those scary ghosts?"

"The two of us have to talk Dad into taking us to town. We'll talk to him tonight and get him to take us tomorrow morning. Then we just have to find the Whitners' address." An easy plan if it worked.

Lucy put her hand on my arm. "Wish I could go with you to help." I wished she could go too, but I didn't want to hurt Ron's feelings by saying that, so I just smiled at her.

I took one of Ron's hands and looked him in the eye again. "Ron, It's really, really important that Dad doesn't know about the ghosts or the note or anything."

"But, Josie, he might help us if he knew. We could tell him about the ghosts and..." Ron started.

I interrupted. "Tell Dad about ghosts. What did he say to you about ghosts?"

Ron stood still for a moment. "Nah, I guess he wouldn't believe us. He'd laugh again."

We planned to meet Lucy the day after tomorrow once Boss Whitner got the note and the plan got under way. I crossed my fingers.

That night at dinner I made the pitch to Dad. "We could look around Kessler. We could have lunch downtown. Maybe we could see a movie or something. Then we could go back to the library. I need some new books to read, and Ron does too." I used my most sincere voice. "We've stayed here all this time. We need a day in town."

I gave more reasons, just in case. "Grandma could have some peace and quiet for a whole day. We'll have fun, Dad." I felt guilty, even though I didn't tell any lies, at least not technically.

"Ron, do you want to go to town with your sister?"

"Oh, yeah, Dad. We'll have lots of fun." I gave Ron a don't-overdo-it kick under the table.

Dad looked at Grandma. "What do you think, Mom?"

I held my breath, afraid of Grandma volunteering to go along and watch us.

Grandma looked hard at me, then she smiled gently. "Josie acts very responsibly. If she wants to take Ronnie to town, she can certainly handle taking him. A day to myself sounds very nice."

I slowly let out my breath. I'm pretty sure Grandma suspected something, but she trusted me to handle things. I didn't know if that made me feel better or worse.

"I leave pretty early, guys. I'll only call you once."

"No problem. Right, Josie?" Ron grinned at me.

"You bet." So far, so good.

Chapter 10

I jumped up when Dad called the next morning. I put on clean shorts and a shirt with a collar instead of a tee. I'd written the note to Boss Whitner on the computer last night. I nervously tucked it in the pocket of my shorts.

"Where to first?" Dad turned the car away from the big trees of Whitner and on to the main highway. We'd already made it through the green tunnel safely.

Ron looked at me.

"I think we'll go to the library first."

"Okay, I have some errands to run for your grandmother, but I'll drop you two at the library first." He kept his eyes on the road. "If you need me for anything, go upstairs to the conference room." He looked at his watch. "You can find me there in an hour or so. Here's lunch money for both of you, Josie."

He handed me the bills, and I tucked them in my pocket with the note, then quickly transferred them to my other pocket.

"You'll need to meet me back at the library no later than four o'clock. I don't want to have to wait, kids. Josie, you have your watch?"

"Yes. No waiting. We're going to look at the town after lunch, but we'll come back on time."

Dad drove up in front of a red brick building with wide cement stairs that rose high to a big door.

"Four o'clock now." He frowned.

Dad sounded like he wasn't happy about leaving us. He seemed worried, but I didn't know why. I'd taken Ron to the library a lot of times in Tuscaloosa. I held Ron's hand and we went up the stairs.

The library felt cool inside and the air smelled comfortingly of old books. I took Ron straight to the front desk. I wanted to finish this before Dad came back

"We'd like to look at the phone directories, please."

The librarian smiled at Ron and me and directed us to a nearby shelf. I hoped we could find Homer Whitner listed in the book, copy the address and get out of there.

The Kessler phone book looked about a half-inch thick. Ron followed as I walked to a table where I rifled through the directory to the W's and Whitner. No luck. No Homer, no James, nothing. An unlisted number, I bet.

"We have to think of another way, Ron."

"Why don't we just ask that nice lady." He pointed at the librarian who'd helped us.

Little kids go right to the simplest answer. Well, why not? We couldn't wander around all day looking.

"Ron, you're right. That's what we'll do. Let me do the talking, though." Ron nodded.

We stood in line behind two ladies, each with an armload of books to check out. Finally, the librarian turned to Ron and me with that nice smile.

"Excuse me, I need some information."

Not what I intended to say.

"I'll help you if I can." Her voice sounded kind. I looked at her closely. She reminded me of Grandma. She had the same patient look around her eyes.

"My brother and I live in Whitner this summer, in the old Whitner house." Now she'd know us. That might turn into a problem.

"Of course. Mr. Wallace's children. He's researching the Whitner Iron Company, isn't he?" Her smile grew bigger and kinder than before. "What a nice man."

"Yes, ma'am. We really like the old Whitner house. Have you ever visited?" I acted as polite as possible while wanting to rush through. We needed to go before Dad got back.

"No, I haven't, but I'm sure you like the house. Are you doing research too?" A man stood in line behind us. I needed to get to the point.

"Well, yes, some. Our Daddy told us that the Whitners, the ones who used to live there, live in Kessler. We'd like to just look at the place they live now to see if, if...," I ran out of steam.

"To see if they live in just as nice a place now," Ron piped in. I started to glare at him, but after all, I'd muffed my chance.

To my surprise, she smiled again. "You just want to get a look at the house and not bother the Whitners?

I can see why you're curious about them. My parents used to talk about them all the time. They were the wealthiest family around. I'd love to see the house in Whitner."

"You can come to see us," Ron said. I elbowed him.

"Well now, thank you. That's very nice. We'll see." She pulled a pad of paper over and began writing. "Here's the address. You need directions?"

"Yes, ma'am." We said it together.

I kept myself from snatching the paper out of her hand. Both Ron and I thanked her again. Then I grabbed his hand and rushed him out of the library into the bright sunlight.

I glanced at the paper with the directions the librarian had given us. "Go right as you leave the library, seven blocks to Center Street."

We just had to stay on this street and walk to Center Street.

The sun beat down on us for the seven long blocks. I got really hot. Ron bounced right along. This time I felt grateful for his energy. He didn't complain once.

I was sweaty and tired by the time we got to Center Street, but Ron looked like he'd just left the house. I looked at the paper again.

"Turn left. Two blocks down on Center. Turn right on Whitner Street." A street all their own.

The big trees on Center Street eased the heat. The shade brought my energy back.

On the short street of Whitner, the trees looked

bigger and sat close together, like a forest with a street in the middle.

I tried not to think of Homer Whitner and what he'd done to Lucy. He be an old, old man, maybe too sick and weak to come to Whitner. Then what?

A large white house loomed through the trees at the end of the street. It appeared still, empty, and spooky. I felt for the note in my pocket.

"What now, Josie?" Ron tugged at my hand.

"Well, we better not just go up and ring the bell. Let's go back to Center Street. I think I saw an alley."

"I'm kind of scared." Ron edged behind me.

"You want to wait out on Center Street, Ron? I'd understand. But I've got to do this." I trembled, but I had to give Boss Whitner the note. Then we'd get out of there fast.

"I'm staying with you." He clenched his fists, brave for such a little guy.

We found the alley and walked down. No other houses except the Whitner house occupied the alley. We stood behind the corner of a large garage and peeked at the backyard. Giant oak trees grew close together through the back yard.

We picked our way toward the house from one wide tree trunk to another. As we got closer, I saw a man stretched out in a chaise lounge just outside the house.

I led Ron to the last large oak, the one closest to the house. The man in the chaise appeared extremely old. A brown and green plaid coverlet protected his legs, and he wore a shapeless old brown sweater.

Wrinkles covered his face and the hands that lay still on the coverlet. I thought he slept.

Boss Whitner. I wanted to turn and run, but I thought of Lucy and Aggie.

I whispered to Ron, "Stay here. I'm going to put the note in his lap. Be ready to get out of here fast."

"Josie," he whispered back. "Let me do it. You know how I can sneak with no sounds. Let me do it. Please."

I hesitated. He always showed up behind me out of nowhere without a sound. I can't move across a room without making a racket. "All right. But if you see an eye open or if he moves at all, run hard as you can. The man looks old and helpless, but don't be fooled."

"I know. I will."

I held my breath as Ron crept soundlessly out toward the old man. I shouldn't have let him go. What if the old man woke and grabbed Ron?

Then Ron gently placed the note on the coverlet between the old man's hands. He whirled and raced toward me like a boy on fire.

He gasped for breath when I caught him in my arms. "Did I do good, Josie?" he whispered between gasps.

"You did great, Ron. Just fantastic." I felt like crying with relief.

I sneaked one last look toward the old man as we backed away from trunk to trunk. Awake, he fumbled in his sweater pocket with one gnarled hand and held the note in the other. The hand came out of his pocket with a pair of gold-rimmed glasses.

Time to get out of there. Ron and I clasped hands, and we took off back up the alley. We didn't stop running until we went two blocks down Center Street toward town. We stood leaning over, hands on our knees until we could breathe normally again.

Then we walked slowly toward downtown Kessler.

"Hey, Josie." Ron stopped me. "We did it, didn't we?"

"We sure did, Ronnie. There's no way I could have done it without you. I absolutely couldn't have."

As we walked along, I imagined the old man reading the note:

"Homer Whitner, we know what you did in the infirmary all those years ago. Come back to the scene of your crimes in Whitner at ten o'clock Monday morning or we will give our proof to the newspapers. Signed, a friend."

Chapter 11

"You all done great," Lucy said, after Ron and I told her the details of our trip to Kessler. "Think he gonna' come?"

Ron and I looked at each other. Once we left the note, I never considered that he might not come. After all this, though, he had to.

"I sure hope so, Lucy. He will come, won't he?"

"He'll come." Ron said. "Can I wait there with you?"

Lucy shook her head. "Better not, Ronnie. Better not."

I agreed. I didn't know what to expect. "I wish you could, but I don't think that's a good idea."

"Why? I want to go with you and see what happens. I won't get in the way. Promise!"

"You're a great help, Ron. Look how you helped in Kessler. But this time I need you to help by staying home. You stay with Grandma. If I'm not home by lunchtime, you can tell her where to find me. She can call Dad for help. You have to stick around the house to tell her in case I don't come home."

I knelt to look in Ron's eyes. "You have an

important job, Ron. Can you handle it?"

We might truly need help. I hadn't thought much about the danger before. That old man had killed two people that we knew of. People don't change. I hoped I wouldn't have to get near him, but everything depended on Aggie and the doctor.

I knew Ron didn't want to give in, but he did. "I guess," he finally sighed. "But I want to know what happens with the ghosts and the old man. You better tell me."

"I will tell you every thing that happens. I promise. I never broke a promise to you, did I?" I hoped to tell him a very short story. I dreaded going near the infirmary again.

Ron lay back, looked up into the old oak, and listened carefully while Lucy and I talked about Boss Whitner's visit on Monday.

"So what do we do after he gets there, Lucy? Do we just sit back and watch? Do we need to do something to help?" I wanted her to say that I should stay back and that she'd stay with me.

"He come and he see them ghosts, they take care of him, I reckon. He don't see them then this ain't the way to get us home. We go back and we try again. Do something else."

"Do you think he'll see them? I can't think what else we could do, can you?"

"This seemed like the right thing. Don't you go worrying. This plan gonna work. I feel it." Her voice held a note of hope.

"Me, too." I wished I felt as sure as I sounded.

At dinner that night, Dad said, "Tomorrow's Sunday, Josie. You ready to show me the neighborhood?"

I'd forgotten all about that. Would he see or feel the ghosts if I showed him the infirmary? Well, if he did he might help, or he might make me stay home with Ron. Although scared, I wanted to go to the infirmary Monday at ten.

"Sure, Dad. You want to see anything special?" I'd need to keep him away from Lucy. He wouldn't see her as a ghost, but I didn't know what he'd do if he saw her in Whitner.

"Is the infirmary still there? I'd like to see where the little girl died." I nodded like a dummy. "I can't find a record of the doctor that treated her. Maybe I can find his name on a door or something. If I can find him, he might help me understand why, after her death, the plant closed and the families left Whitner."

I almost choked on my tuna sandwich. Ron fumbled with his fork and dropped it on the floor with a bang.

I took a long drink of my iced tea. "You need to see the Ford house and the schoolhouse first. You'd get a real feel for the people of Whitner. Then we could go to the infirmary if there's time. Is that all right?" I still wasn't sure I wanted him go inside the infirmary.

"That sounds like a good plan. I've got most of the history of the plant itself, but I can't get a handle on the people. Let's do it that way. Good thinking, Josie." He smiled.

Chapter 12

I sneaked Ron out the back door the next morning after breakfast. He dashed down to tell Lucy to hide. We couldn't have Dad see her. Ron came back soon and nodded to me. He'd told Lucy.

Grandma kept Dad busy with chores through the morning. We ate lunch, our big meal, late on Sundays. Grandma fixed fried chicken and mashed potatoes. I knew we'd leave late. Dark might fall before Dad and I got to the infirmary.

After lunch, Dad said, "Let's go, Josie. "Where to first?"

We went to the Ford house. I didn't have to stall him. He took his time, jotting notes on a pad and walked around the yard mumbling to himself. "Probably a typical steel worker's home. Very interesting."

I bit my tongue to keep from telling him the stories Lucy told me about the Fords. He'd love hearing them. We spent a good long time at the school. Seeing the old desks still there surprised Dad. He inspected each, inside and out, but didn't find anything but dust.

"I need to look into this. I necd to know when the

school closed. Look at that slate blackboard. I can't believe they didn't move all this to use elsewhere."

"Dad, let's stop at the post office." I tried to put off the infirmary as long as I could.

"No, it's getting late. I want to get to the infirmary before dark. Since they left furniture in the schoolhouse, maybe they left files in the infirmary. Did you see anything in there?"

I shook my head. He practically skipped along the road past the commissary. I bit my fingernails.

The white building looked just the same, but it seemed to glow in the setting sun. I wanted no part of seeing ghosts now. I hung back as Dad climbed the few steps to the door.

"Darn, the door's locked. Have you looked in the windows?" He didn't wait for an answer, but made his way down the steps and over to one of the windows.

Locked? Who locked it? Was it possible that someone or something didn't want Dad in there? Lucy? The ghosts?

He rubbed on the dusty glass of the window and looked inside. "Can't see anything. Too dark. I'll have to get a key and come back another time." He turned from the window. "I probably won't find old records anyway."

We walked back toward the post office and home.

"For some reason, I still have a feeling that getting into the infirmary might help me understand Whitner. I'm not sure why."

He didn't talk the rest of the way home. Neither did I.

Chapter 13

"Well, Josie. Early for you, isn't it?" Grandma said when she saw me come down the stairs Monday morning as Ron chomped on Sweet and Crunchies at the kitchen table. He looked at me hard. I smiled at him. Butterflies danced in my stomach. I could eat only a few bites of my Crunchies. I said goodbye to Grandma and Ron and started on my way.

Lucy and I had planned to meet at nine o'clock. We wanted time to hide near the infirmary and keep watch for Boss Whitner. What happened once he got there, who knew? Maybe nothing. Maybe he wouldn't even come.

Lucy perched on the edge of the post office steps. "Are you ready, Lucy?" I asked. She raised her eyebrows. Most likely she felt jittery too.

"Been thinking. We hide in that big bunch of bottlebrush growing right off the road," she said. "Be a good place to see from."

We started down the road toward the infirmary.

"You daddy look all around? He see anything?"

"He couldn't get into the infirmary. Someone locked the door."

"They didn't want him in there, I reckon." She looked down at the road. "You daddy a nice man?"

"Sure. Dad's great!" I wondered why she asked.

"You lucky." Lucy must have missed her parents all these years. I hoped she'd get to see them again soon.

The bottlebrush made a perfect hiding place. The white flowers and green leaves hid us well.

Lucy flattened a section right in the middle of the weeds with her feet. I stomped the stems with my sneakers. Soon we made room to sit. Down in the crushed space, the plants grew high enough to hide us completely. The stems tickled my legs, but we could see the road and the infirmary clearly.

We didn't talk. We both stared down the road toward the commissary and batted away the gnats that circled us. We waited what seemed like more than an hour, but probably wasn't very long.

We heard the car before we saw it, a loud sound in the quiet summer air. The car raised a cloud of dust as it moved down the red dirt road toward the infirmary. The butterflies in my stomach moved wildly, trying to beat their way out. I clutched Lucy's hand tightly.

The long black car with dark tinted windows rolled to a stop right in front of the infirmary door about ten feet from where we hid. After the dust settled, the driver's door slowly opened. A man got out stiffly. He wore a dark suit in spite of the summer heat. He looked old, but not old enough for Homer Whitner. He hurried around and opened the back door, reached inside, then backed up.

"I can get out the door myself. I ain't feeble as all that, you know!" The voice sounded strong, but scratchy.

The old man slowly pulled himself out of the back seat. I recognized the withered face from Kessler. Boss Whitner. He struggled to his feet and leaned heavily on a black cane, both his gnarled hands clutching the shiny gold handle. I couldn't take my eyes away from the cane. I looked at Lucy. She stared at the man with her eyes wide. She clutched my hand so tight it hurt.

Boss Whitner glared around him with his cold piercing eyes. A scowl turned the corners of his mouth down.

The first man was the son, I felt sure. Both wore dark suits as if headed for a funeral.

I wondered what the son thought of his father. Lucy said he stood by when his father killed the doctor. Was he as dangerous as his father? I felt dizzy at the thought.

"Mr. Whitner?" I heard Dad's voice. "I'm surprised to see you way out here." He shook hands with the son. "Is this your father? I'm glad he's feeling better. Good morning, Sir."

Boss Whitner seemed to rumble something as he glanced fiercely at my father.

So focused on watching the Whitners, I missed seeing Dad come up the road. Why did he come? No, I didn't care why he came. I felt relieved and safer.

The son took a step toward Dad. "Wallace? You give my dad that note?"

"Note? I'm afraid I don't know about a note. I

wanted to look in this building as part of my research." Dad gestured toward the infirmary. "So I brought back a skeleton key this morning. Darn thing's locked."

"Ridiculous!" Boss Whitner sneered. The old man determinedly made his way to the building and stumped step by step with his cane up to the door. He rattled the knob.

"I'll get the door, Papa," the son said. He hovered close behind his father, as if afraid the older man might fall. But Boss Whitner hit at him with the cane and opened the door himself.

The men, including my father crowded into the place. I could hear windows screeching up. I didn't know the windows moved. Then through the open window above us, we heard Boss Whitner's scratchy voice, soft at first, "Aggie?" then much louder, "Aggie?"

"Now," Lucy said.

I pushed at the bottlebrush stems and led the way out, to the door of the infirmary. Lucy crowded beside me in the doorway. I stared in.

Aggie sat on the side of the bed, spotlighted by a ray of sunlight slanting through a window. One of her arms stretched out toward her father. Boss Whitner gaped and held a trembling hand toward the girl.

Dad stood back by the door watching Boss Whitner. The son huddled against the wall looking at his father like he thought the old man completely mad.

"Aggie, that you?" The old man's voice grew stronger now.

"Nobody's there, Papa. Aggie's gone," the son

said. He reached out to put his hand on his father's shoulder, then changed his mind and jerked his hand back.

In a soft musical tone, Aggie spoke. I'd never heard her speak. I'd only heard her cry. "Daddy, Daddy, what did you do?"

I slipped into the room and stood close to my father. He looked at me and raised his eyebrows, then he put an arm over my shoulders. He said nothing. Maybe he looked at the little girl, or maybe just at the bed.

Lucy came in and marched toward Aggie. I clasped Dad's hand and watched Lucy and Aggie.

Boss Whitner gaped at Lucy. His voice wailed, louder than ever. "You! No, no not you! You're dead!"

Boss backed away from Lucy, stumbling, his cane clattering to the floor. His raspy gasps for breath sounded loud in the small room. His son stared at him. He didn't seem able to move.

Just at that moment, the doctor loomed in the doorway of the back room. He glared at Homer Whitner. His ghastly smile terrified me. I huddled closer to my father.

As if Boss Whitner could sense the doctor's presence, he turned sluggishly and moaned deep in his throat. He staggered for a moment, grasped his hand to his chest, then he crumpled to the floor.

The doctor dipped his head once as if in satisfaction. His smile turned smug. He looked with contempt at the withered old man, Boss Whitner. Then he looked up at Aggie. He gave a quick nod of his head and faded away.

Whitner's son knelt beside the old man. He shook his head slowly.

Dad gave me a questioning look. "Are you all right, Josie?"

"I'm okay, Dad. Go see about the old man, okay?"

Dad looked hard at me again, then stepped over to kneel with the son by the fallen old man.

Lucy came over and took my hand. She looked into my eyes. "We going now, Josie. Aggie, she ready. The doc, he gone."

I wanted to beg her to stay. In the short time I'd known her, she'd turned into my good friend, an important part of my life. Without her, I'd feel lost. But she couldn't stay. We planned all this so that they could go.

"I'll miss you, Lucy. You'll always be my friend." I choked back tears.

"And you mine, but you gonna have a whole bunch of friends. I know for sure. I'm gonna miss you, Josie. I thank you, and Aggie thank you." She squeezed my hand.

We went back to Aggie, still holding hands. With her other hand Lucy took Aggie's. Aggie smiled at me. The two girls faded away. My hand grasped nothing. Tears started to stream down my face. I swiped them away with the back of my hand. I felt a hole in place of my heart. Suddenly I grew aware of what had happened in the room.

"He's dead," the son said as he stood. "What did he see?" He looked down at his father. "Being here must have brought back memories of Aggie. He seemed sure that he saw her here. His memories killed him, I guess."

My father rose and came over to me. He looked at me curiously, then put his arm around my shoulders again. Then he looked up at Boss Whitner's son. "I'm so sorry, Mr. Whitner."

"He'd lived a long time, Mr. Wallace. I guess his time came after all these years."

"I'll go back to the house and call an ambulance if that's all right with you." Dad still held me tightly.

"Very kind of you. Very kind."

"Come on, Josie." Dad led me toward the door.

Outside, I stood sobbing. Dad put his arms around me and waited. I held my breath to make myself calm down, then said, "Daddy, did Mr. Whitner really die? Nobody meant for him to die."

Had I caused this old man to die? Did he have to die before the other three found peace? I felt stunned.

Dad took tissues from his pocket and put them in my hand. I wiped my eyes, then blew my nose. He hugged me. "Josie, the man was very old. I'm sorry you had to see him die."

I stopped crying. I held my breath so I wouldn't start again. "Dad, there's a lot I have to tell you. I don't know if you'll believe me, but I have to tell you everything. It'll take a long time."

"I want to hear. Right now we have to get home to make that call. We'll have a long talk soon. I have questions and there's something I want to tell you, too." We walked down the road toward the house.

Chapter 14

My father had to go into Kessler early the next morning to speak with the authorities about Boss Whitner's death. It took all day.

Ron shot questions at me that morning. I tried to answer as much as I thought a seven-year-old could handle, promising more later. Then I spent most of the day sitting under the oak where Lucy and I had talked. I felt close to her there.

I wanted to organize in my mind exactly what to tell Dad. I hoped I could lay out Lucy's story in a clear way. Whether he believed me or not, I'd feel better once I told him everything.

At the dinner table with Ron and Grandma, Dad kept the conversation as normal as possible. After dinner, Dad and I went to the front porch. Outside, grassy smells perfumed the air. The night insects rasped loud songs in the warm night. Everything seemed ordinary. Except that everything still felt strange.

We sat quietly for a few minutes, then Dad spoke

first. "Who was the girl who came into the infirmary with you yesterday, Josie?"

I jerked my head up to look at him. He had seen Lucy. "Old Mr. Whitner seemed afraid of her. Do you know why?"

"Lucy, my friend, my good friend. I've met her every day since we got here. You'd like her. And yes, I know why Boss Whitner feared her. I felt relieved I could finally tell him the truth. "Dad, did you see anyone else in the infirmary, besides the Whitners, I mean?"

"Well." He rubbed his hand over his face. "I thought I saw.... I'm not really sure. Two other people, I thought....but not really. I thought I saw a little girl and a man. Homer Whitner saw them. They shocked and upset him. I think that's why he died."

"Yes, I think so." Dad saw the ghosts! "I feel bad Mr. Whitner had to die, but, you know, he had done some very bad things." I fought back tears when I thought about the man falling dead.

Dad leaned toward me and patted my knee. "Can you tell me what he did? What made him bad? I'd like to hear about your friend and those other two people I saw, if you can tell me."

"I can tell you everything, but I don't know if you'll believe me. It's a long story."

"I have an abundance of time, Josie. Tell me, please." He settled back in the wicker chair to listen, and I told him everything that Lucy had told me. I even told him about delivering the note with Ron, expecting consequences for that.

When I finished, he sat silently for a long time.

"You don't believe me, do you?" I didn't really care. I felt drained, but I also felt an enormous relief.

"No, I think...I do believe you." He leaned forward to put his hand on my shoulder. "I'm sorry you felt you had to go through that by yourself, Sweetheart. It's a very strange story. I might not have believed it a few days ago."

Dad leaned back in his wicker chair again with a sigh. "I went to the infirmary yesterday morning because someone came to see me. I'd asked around Kessler, you know, for anyone who used to live here in Whitner before the plant closed."

Dad dug in his pocket and pulled out a slip of paper and looked at it. "A certain...George Ford, Jr. lived in Whitner as a boy. He told me an unbelievable story. It seems George's father said he saw the ghost of a girl who had died in the town reservoir not long after young Agatha Whitner died. George said several of the Ford's neighbors saw the girl around Whitner. The encounter unnerved George's family badly. When the plant closed later, they happily left Whitner, as did the neighbors. The Fords moved to Kessler."

"Lucy told me about going to see Mr. Ford. That's when she found out about herself."

"I believe they all saw Lucy, Josie. Though, when I talked to George Ford, I'm afraid I didn't believe him. The story seemed outlandish. At least, I thought so until my experience in the infirmary."

We sat together and listened to the crickets chirping and the occasional loud cicada song. My heart still ached, but I felt more at ease than I had since we drove into Whitner.

Finally, Dad spoke. "Amazing as it seems, I think your friend Lucy may have inadvertently caused the mass exodus from the town."

We sat without talking for a while longer in the summer night.

Then Dad said, "Josie, I think we better keep all this to ourselves. I won't mention it in my findings."

"No problem, Dad. Who'd believe us anyway? I only wish no one had to die to solve Lucy's problem."

Dad shook his head. "So do I. So do I. But Whitner's death brought rest to the others. From what I saw today, I think his death may have brought peace to his son also."

We fell silent again for a time. Then Dad tapped his chin with an index finger. "Maybe when I have time to write that novel...." His voice trailed off.

Then he got up and pulled me out of my chair. "Come on. Time for bed." And hand in hand we went into the house.

Ron couldn't talk to me about anything but the ghosts for the rest of our summer in Whitner. He asked me a million questions about how the ghosts looked. I must have described Boss Whitner to him ten times.

Now that we're home, Ron's busy with school and friends. He's playing soccer for the first time this year. I think maybe he's forgotten what happened last summer.

Sometimes I think I'd like to forget about it myself, I don't think I ever will. I have pushed it out of my mind for now. There's schoolwork to do and books to read. And there's my best friend, Sally. We laugh together and talk about everything. Joan and Nancy, too. We hang out at the park, or one of our houses.

No, I'm not surrounded by a whole bunch of friends like Lucy said, but that's three good friends. Enough for now. I still like to spend time alone occasionally, but I enjoy people more than I used to. Maybe I'm just growing up.

But every time I laugh and every time I sing silly songs with the girls, I think of the summer with Lucy. I'll always miss her.

To order additional copies of
Ghosts of Whitner

Name _____

Address _____

_____

_____

$9.95 x _____ copies =   _____

Sales Tax   _____
(Texas residents add 8.25% sales tax)

Please add $2.75 postage and handling/book   _____

Total amount due: _____

Please send check or money order for books to:

WordWright.biz, Inc.
***WordWright* Business Park**
46561 State Highway 118
Alpine, Texas 79830

For a complete catalog of books,
visit our site at
http://www.WordWright.biz

Printed in the United States
43970LVS00006B/34-39

9 781932 196474